I

A Play

by George Cameron Grant

A SAMUEL FRENCH ACTING EDITION

SAMUEL FRENCH

FOUNDED 1830

Copyright © 2012 by George Cameron Grant

ISBN 978-0-87440-331-2   Printed in U.S.A.   #B1126

MUSIC USE NOTE

IMPORTANT BILLING AND CREDIT REQUIREMENTS

PUSH was first performed Sunday, July 31st, 2010, at the Hudson Guild Theatre in New York City as a participant in the Strawberry One Act Festival. It was named a Festival semi-finalist, and was performed again on August 3, 2010. Both performances were directed by Liz Amadio, with sound and lights by Zach Pizza, garnering Best Actress (Emma Charap) and Best Director (Liz Amadio) nominations. The cast was as follows:

EVE	Emma Charap
HOODIED FIGURE	Abbey Rowe
BILLY	Ted Kolsby
MOTHER	Hank Morris
FATHER	Vincent Bandille
FEMALE TEENAGER #1	Kacy Hopkins / Anaridia Burgos
FEMALE TEENAGER #2	Abbey Rowe
MALE TEENAGER	Wesley Tunison
JAVIER	Francisco Huergo

Encore performances of *PUSH* were performed Friday, March 2, 2012 and Sunday, March 4, 2012 at the Hudson Guild Theatre in NYC, as a participant in the Strawberry One Act Festival. Performances were directed by Liz Amadio, with sound and lights by Zach Pizza, with Sarah Jones as the Stage Manager. The cast was as follows:

EVE	Emma Charap
HOODIED FIGURE	Abbey Rowe
BILLY	Ted Kolsby
MOTHER	Hank Morris
FATHER	Vincent Bandille
FEMALE TEENAGER #1	Alana Tyrrell
FEMALE TEENAGER #2	Abbey Rowe
MALE TEENAGER	Edwin Morel
JAVIER	Francisco Huergo

Eastside Side Players of Madison, Wisconsin

The Eastside Players of Madison (WI) East High School participated in the Wisconsin High School Theatre Festival in Fall of 2012 with a production of *PUSH*, produced and directed by Paul Milisch.

The cast: Scout Slava-Ross, Liam Sunde, Molly Riedemann, Ted Huwe, Joseph Garcia Menocal, Lexie Callen, Zoe Kjos, Anna Mickle, Max Alvarado, Evan Kind, Joe Klafka. Understudies: Anna Cohen, Seth Campbell, Michelle Morency, Cosmos Nikimos, Laura Bessenecker.

The crew: Emma Rankin-Utevsky (Stage Manager), Michelle Morency (Asst. Stage Manager), Laura Bessenecker & Anna Cohen (Run Crew), Cosmos Nikimos (Sound Operator), Seth Campbell (Light Operator).

The production advanced through the festival to the State level, and the production received an All-State Award. Scout Slava-Ross was also awarded an Outstanding Actor Award for her portrayal of Eve.

The Eastside Players dedicated their production to everyone who has ever been hurt, alienated, or generalized by other people's words, and the production involved collaboration with East High's WORDS HURT club as well as the LGBQT support staff of the Madison Metropolitan School District.

Anna Cohen will be performing *CHRISTMAS EVE AT THE ESPLANADE*, the original monologue which evolved into *PUSH*, featured in the back of this book, in the upcoming Wisconsin Forensics Festival.

Now in Preparation!

PUSH is currently being adapted for the screen by the Film and Drama Department of the Frank Sinatra School of the Arts, Astoria, New York. With the intention of creating a "tool for tolerance," *PUSH* will be a film made *by* students *for* students.

CHARACTERS

EVE
BILLY
MOTHER
FATHER
2 TEENAGE GIRLS
TEENAGE BOY
JAVIER
HOODIED FIGURE

AUTHOR'S NOTE

Bullying, sexual harassment, intimidation, and violence can be an every-day occurrence in a child's life. Whether originating in the school, neighborhood, or even their own home, the consequential dysfunction and depression can be disturbing, sometimes dangerous, even deadly. *PUSH* attempts to engage these unfortunate realities of childhood head on and unvarnished. No doubt it will incite debate. Hopefully, it will also inspire communication, compassion, and connectivity between students and their parents, teachers, and loved ones. I urge you to examine *PUSH* for yourself, then hope you will be compelled to encourage your school, theater, library, place of worship, or community organization to present the play. Whether staged, or as a simple reading, my wish is that *PUSH* will become a useful "tool for tolerance" in ensuring every child's right to live, learn, and love, in a safe environment.

ONE BULLIED CHILD IS ONE TOO MANY!

– George Cameron Grant
2011

ACKNOWLEDGEMENTS

My deepest appreciation goes out to the following:
Your generosity of time, talent, insight, stubbornness, encouragement and
unconditional love, helped bring **PUSH** *into the light, and helps keep me out of*
the dark.

Richard Abramowitz
Liz Amadio
Father Douglas Arcoleo
Jeff Baltimore / XL Graphics, NYC
Vincent Bandille
Anaridia Burgos
Donna Finn
Van Dirk Fisher
Louise Freymann
Kacy Hopkins
Francisco Huergo
Robert Kamlot
Ted Kolsby
Hank Morris
Abbey Rowe
Wesley Tunison
Father Nestor Watin
Larry Winer

and especially to my daughters

Elizabeth & Jenna

A special note of gratitude must go out to
Miss Emma Charap,
whose courage and trust inspired me to write
CHRISTMAS EVE AT THE ESPLANADE,
the original monologue from which **PUSH** *evolved.*
Emma magnificently originated the role of Eve on December 14, 2010,
at The Producers Club in NYC.

PUSH
*is dedicated to all adolescent and teenage victims
of anger, abuse, bullying, ignorance, and exploitation.*

(Scene: A dimly lit Bronx subway station, yellow warning stripe butting the edge of the stage...)

(Time: 5am, Christmas Eve.)

(At rise: **EVE**, *a girl of sixteen, sits huddled in a barely lit corner of the station upstage right, sound asleep, hands stuffed into the pockets of the way-too-big, red varsity jacket she wears, the name* **BILLY** *embroidered on it, red wool cap pulled over the hair covering her shoulders. The approaching thunder of an oncoming train is heard, and as it passes, flickering lights illuminate the stirring* **EVE**, *while also revealing a* **BLACK-HOODIED FIGURE**, *seen only from behind, lowering an object into a red trash can downstage left. As the roar of the train fades and the station returns to shadows,* **EVE** *nuzzles deeper into the corner, just as a clanking of the garbage can is heard. Eyes instantly open,* **EVE** *springs to her feet, hands emerging from the jacket, one holding an opening box cutter, extended and ready for anything, as the* **FIGURE** *withdraws...)*

EVE. Who's there? I know you're hiding behind that pole, so you might as well come out where I can...*(cautiously approaching the trash can)*...I'm warning you, I've got a sharp blade in my hand and I'm not afraid to use it, so if you're thinking of trying anything, you'd better... *(squinting toward the sound of running footsteps)* ...jeez, it's a - hey, come back, I thought you were just another creep trying to - really, you don't have to run away!... *(Closing the box cutter, she pockets it, extending empty hands.)* ...I put it away, see? I'm not going to hurt you, I swear. Look, if you're hungry, I've got half a sandwich here somewhere...*(extending a wrinkled bag she removes from her jacket pocket)*...see, here it is, now come back! Hey!...*(stuffing bag back into the jacket pocket)* ...gone...

(looks up) ...damn it, Billy, are you happy now? You've got me scarin' the hell out of some kid who's probably more frightened than *I* am! I don't mean to yell at you, but everything's such a freakin' mess down here. I'm a mess, Mom and Dad are a mess, it's all turned to crap, and I don't know what to do or who else to turn to, so you're just gonna' have to put up with this, *OK!* *(She slowly returns to the corner.)* I remember the exact moment you told me. Thanksgiving morning, in front of the TV, right before the parade came on. I knew you'd been holding something back, keeping something from me, but I never would have guessed...

*(Lights up on **BILLY**, Eve's brother, sitting on the floor, up center stage, white T-shirt and jeans, pen in hand, a well-worn, opened notebook in his lap, as he turns to her.)*

BILLY. ...I'm in love!

EVE. Oh.

BILLY. Did you hear me, Eve? I said I'm in love.

(She crosses stage and sits beside him.)

EVE. I heard you.

BILLY. And that's all you have to say?

EVE. I'm sorry, Billy - look, that's great - I'm happy for you.

BILLY. It would be nice if you meant it.

EVE. I *do* mean it.

BILLY. But?

EVE. Come on, Billy, you're *always* in love.

BILLY. That's not true.

EVE. Sure it is. You daydream about it, talk about it when you're *not* daydreaming about it - *you were just singing about it in the shower* - I'll bet anything you're working on some kind of love poem in that notebook of yours right now.

(He self-consciously shuts the notebook.)

BILLY. So what's wrong with that?

EVE. Nothing, if you weren't always getting your butt kicked by it.

BILLY. Love's a risk, sis, sometimes you have to push yourself to take a chance.

EVE. I wouldn't know.

BILLY. How could you?

EVE. Why would I want to? All I know about love is Mom and Dad - and you - so forgive me if I'm not exactly in a rush to find out for myself.

BILLY. *That* was kinda' mean.

EVE. But the truth! You're the ones who are supposed to be setting a good example, and so far you're all doing a pretty crummy job.

BILLY. Gee, thanks.

EVE. Come on, Billy, you know the way you are.

BILLY. This is *different*, sis.

EVE. Whatever you say.

BILLY. It is.

EVE. Alright, I believe you.

BILLY. This is serious, Evie, this is for real.

EVE. And all the others were—

BILLY. Me just trying to be somebody else.

(*She hugs him.*)

EVE. I love that somebody else, I don't ever want to lose him.

BILLY. Don't worry, you won't.

EVE. I hope not.

BILLY. I'm still Billy, only this Billy's finally doing *what* he really wants, with *who* he really wants, not who and what everyone else *thinks* he should really want.

EVE. So who *does* this Billy really want? It's Jessica, right?

BILLY. Jessica?

EVE. Then it's got to be Deborah Spellman, I've seen you two hanging out at the—

BILLY. No!

EVE. No?

BILLY. She's just a friend.

EVE. Annie Hayes?

BILLY. Uh-uh.

EVE. Betsy Callahan.

BILLY. Think you'd better give up.

EVE. Well, do I know who it is or not?

BILLY. No.

EVE. Then who is it? What's her name?

(He turns away.)

Billy?

BILLY. What?

EVE. What's wrong?

BILLY. Nothing.

EVE. Hey, this is *me* you're talking to, big brother, you never have nothing to say about anything, *especially* on the subject of love, so are you going to tell me her name or—

BILLY. Javier.

EVE. Havi-what?

(He turns to her).

BILLY. Javier. That's...*his* name.

(Standing, **EVE** *walks downstage as spot goes out on* **BILLY.***)*

EVE. Yeah, I know, you kept talking after that, but it had to be ten minutes before I could hear what you were saying, because all I could do was keep playing that name over and over in my head. Javier. Javier. *Javier* – thinking maybe it would somehow change to Jessica, Deborah, Juanita, anything but - Billy, I've never been closer to *anyone*, so how come I didn't know this, never sensed or suspected it, not for a second? I mean, it's not like you didn't go out with girls, plenty of girls, and it's not like any girl you *didn't* go out with wouldn't have killed to go out with you, so how come every time you'd tell me about your dates I never realized there was something off, something wrong? How come it never occurred to me that what was missing in your eyes was what I saw that morning when you said...*the name?* Could it be you never knew it yourself? Maybe you *did* know it, but had to deny your feelings until you found someone you couldn't deny? Or maybe you were just too afraid to say anything because you pretty much knew what everyone's reaction would be.

(A cell phone rings...removing it from the jacket pocket, she stares at the number.)

Well, well, there they are again. They call me *every ten minutes.* Most of the time I don't even answer, but if I do, I rarely make a sound, I only listen.

*(Spotlight on Eve's frantic **MOTHER** downstage right, cell phone in hand, and **FATHER**, sheepishly hovering right behind.)*

MOTHER. Evie, are you there? Evie?

FATHER. Please answer your mother, Evie.

*(**MOTHER** covers the receiver.)*

MOTHER. Anthony, please!

*(**EVE** silently hisses at the phone.)*

I know you can hear me, Evie.

FATHER. What your mother's trying to say is -

MOTHER. She knows what I'm trying to say, now would you please let me handle this...*(back into phone)*...we want you back, baby, we miss you terribly.

FATHER. Listen to your mother, Evie.

MOTHER. We're so sorry for everything that was said, everything that's happened.

EVE. Little freakin' late for that, isn't it, Mother?

MOTHER. You're there!

EVE. Of course I'm here.

FATHER. She spoke to you?

MOTHER. Why don't you ever answer me?

EVE. I just did.

FATHER. What's she saying?

> (**MOTHER** *covers phone.*)

MOTHER. *(to* **FATHER***)* Shhh!...*(back to phone)*...we've been
sick to death with worry.

FATHER. Tell her, Mary.

EVE. Tell me what, Mother?

MOTHER. We want you to come home, baby.

EVE. Oh, that.

FATHER. Can I talk to her, please?

MOTHER. No...*(back to phone)*...we need you, Evie, now more
than ever.

EVE. *(in a whisper)* Blah, blah, blah, blah.

MOTHER. What was that?

EVE. Nothing.

FATHER. Please let me speak to her.

> (*He reaches for the phone, but* **MOTHER** *holds it beyond
> his grasp.*)

> (*over* **MOTHER**'s *shoulder*) We just want you home, Evie,
> *no questions asked!*

EVE. No questions asked?

MOTHER. You heard your father.

EVE. *Hah!*

MOTHER. Evie!

> (**EVE** *snaps the cell phone shut ...blackout on* **PARENTS.***)*

EVE. No questions asked! Big of them, huh? *(She walks to
the platform edge.)* Billy, maybe you already know this,
maybe you don't, but the story's everywhere - TV,
newspapers, radio, all over the freakin' internet. *Teen
subway tragedy! Troubled honor student jumps to his death!*
Troubled! Can you believe that crap? Everyone thinks
they know you, think they know what happened, but

I know the truth, I know what really happened. You didn't jump, not really - you were *pushed!*

(Spotlight on two **TEENAGE GIRLS** *up stage left, both holding stacks of books as they cross.)*

FEMALE TEENAGER #1. Betty said she saw Billy Fortunato with some Spanish guy on City Island. She said they were...*(whispers)*...making out.

FEMALE TEENAGER #2. What? Get the frig outta'—

FEMALE TEENAGER #1. You heard me! Touching each other - kissing -

FEMALE TEENAGER #2. That's bull, I don't believe it.

FEMALE TEENAGER #1. Why would she make that up?

FEMALE TEENAGER #2. Billy Fortunato a freakin' queer?

FEMALE TEENAGER #1. Shhh! Guess who's right behind you.

*(***BILLY***, now wearing the same red varsity jacket and wool cap* **EVE** *wears, notebook in hand, enters light where teenage girls are, passes behind them, then, sensing their stare, turns to face them...they giggle, then turn away just as* **MALE TEENAGER** *enters up stage left, knit cap pulled over his head, faded plaid shirt covering T-shirt and ripped jeans.)*

MALE TEENAGER. Hey faggot!

*(***BILLY*** *turns to him.)*

Yeah, that's right, I'm talkin' to you, got a problem with that, fairy?

*(***BILLY*** *turns to walk away as girls begin to giggle.)*

Oh, and how's your spic boyfriend, faggot?

(Angrily turning toward him, fists clenched, **BILLY** *begins walking in his direction.)*

Uh-oh, faggot's angry, I'm shakin'.

*(***BILLY*** *stops, turns, then begins walking away.)*

Where you runnin', girlie boy, I've got something special here just for you.

(He grabs his crotch as the girls laugh.)

EVE. *Push!*

(Lights out on BOY *and* GIRLS *as* BILLY *walks down-stage right,* EVE *at his side, as lights come back up on* FATHER *and* MOTHER, *sitting angled from each other on red chairs, as if gathered around a table...*FATHER *has a red napkin tucked into his open shirt collar.)*

FATHER. *(rubbing his hands)* Let's eat!

*(*EVE *steps between* BILLY *and their* PARENTS.*)*

EVE. *(whispering)* Billy, you sure about this?

(Nodding, he brushes EVE *to the side.)*

BILLY. Mom, Dad, I've got something very important to tell you.

FATHER. Could it be you're finally pulling your head out of the clouds, out of your ass, and back to getting your old spot on the team?

MOTHER. Anthony!

EVE. Daddy!

FATHER. What'd I say? *What?*

BILLY. That's not important to me.

FATHER. Then I don't give a crap - pass the sweet potatoes.

BILLY. I'm in love.

*(*EVE *backs away to centerstage.)*

FATHER. That so?

BILLY. Yeah, Pop, it is.

FATHER. Where's the butter?

BILLY. But that's...that's not all of it.

(Lights out on the family, as EVE *walks centerstage to the edge.)*

EVE. And then you dropped the bomb.

(Lights back up on a furious FATHER *leaping to his feet, chair flying backwards behind him, being held back by an hysterical* MOTHER *as he lunges at* BILLY.*)*

FATHER. Get the hell out of here, and don't even think of coming back! *Now who's got the freakin' butter?*

BILLY. Dad, I need you to listen -

FATHER. Love! You call that love? That's not love, that's an abomination!

MOTHER. Anthony, please, it's *Thanksgiving.*

FATHER. Oh, that's right, how could I forget?... *(looking upward)* ...Thank you, dear Lord, for making my only son a freakin' faggot - guess you misunderstood when I asked for a *ball*player, *stupid me!*

(BILLY turns to his MOTHER.)

BILLY. Mom, please say something to him.

(MOTHER blesses herself.)

MOTHER. Jesus, Mary and Joseph.

FATHER. *They're* not gonna' help you... *(turning to BILLY)* ...you still here?

BILLY. Why do I have to go anywhere?

(FATHER goes nose to nose with BILLY.)

FATHER. Because you're a freak of nature, an embarrassment, only human beings live in this house and you just lost your membership, now get out of my face, and out of my house before I throw you out!

(MOTHER gets between them.)

MOTHER. For the love of God, Anthony, please stop it, you're gonna' give yourself a stroke.

FATHER. Who gives a crap, I'm already dead... *(Picking up the chair, he sits.)* ...now where the hell is the dark meat? *You know how much I love dark meat!*... *(looking up at a stunned BILLY)* ... Did you hear me, faggot, I said get the hell outta' here!

(BILLY slowly withdraws.)

And don't even think of coming back 'cause I'm changing all the locks first thing in the morning.

EVE. *Push!*

*(lights out on **PARENTS** as **BILLY** runs cross stage left into a spotlight that **JAVIER**, a well-dressed Spanish man in his early 20's, suddenly steps into.)*

JAVIER. I'm going home, Billy.

BILLY. What do you mean, home?

JAVIER. Home. *My* home. Back to Pamplona.

BILLY. When? For how long?

JAVIER. Tomorrow. For good.

BILLY. I don't understand.

JAVIER. I talked to my Uncle about a job back home, and he said yes, he can use me, so...I'm going back.

BILLY. But what about us?

*(**JAVIER** turns away.)*

BILLY. Javier? What about what we have? What we feel? What about... *(He opens notebook, rifling through the pages to one near the end.)* ...what about everything we shared? All the things we shared and said, what *you* said—

JAVIER. I should go.

BILLY. *(pointing to the book)* Here! That afternoon we were in the park when you told me—

JAVIER. I have to go!

BILLY. When you told me that *you loved me.*

JAVIER. This is too much for me, Billy, everything's too crazy, it's - how do you call it - a freaking mess.

BILLY. You wanna' talk about a mess? I can't go home anymore, Javier, how's *that* for a freaking mess?

JAVIER. I don't understand.

BILLY. What don't you understand? I told them.

JAVIER. Told who? Told what?

BILLY. My parents, my sister, I told them – about us.

JAVIER. You *what?*

BILLY. I don't know what I was thinking. I thought they'd understand, maybe even be happy for me.

JAVIER. Why did you do that?

BILLY. I had to tell someone, and if you're not able to tell your own family -

JAVIER. That was a mistake.

(As **JAVIER** *turns away,* **BILLY** *touches his shoulder, spinning him around, then drawing him close.)*

BILLY. We could never be a mistake, besides, look how everything's worked out, there's nothing in my way anymore, I can come with you now.

JAVIER. Come with me?

BILLY. That's right

JAVIER. That's not possible.

BILLY. Of course it is.

JAVIER. No, Billy, it isn't.

BILLY. Why not?

JAVIER. Because.

BILLY. Because?

JAVIER. Because...I don't want you to.

BILLY. I don't understand.

JAVIER. Billy, this – us – can*not* happen where I live.

BILLY. Then don't live there, live *here.*

JAVIER. The plans are already made.

BILLY. Change them, we can live together.

JAVIER. It's too late.

BILLY. No, it isn't, let's take a chance, what do we have to lose?

JAVIER. It's finished, Billy.

BILLY. Why can't we just give it a little time and see what happens? A month? A few weeks?

JAVIER. Goodbye, Billy.

BILLY. No, Javier, wait.

JAVIER. I'm sorry, Billy.

BILLY. *You're* sorry? I have nowhere to go.

JAVIER. That's not my fault.

(Stuffing the notebook in his back pocket, **BILLY** *reaches out and angrily grabs* **JAVIER** *by the collar.)*

BILLY. I love you, Javier.

(Gripping **BILLY**'s *hands,* **JAVIER** *peels them off his collar, shoving him backwards before withdrawing into the darkness.)*

EVE. *Push!*

BILLY. Wait!

*(***BILLY*** begins to follow* **JAVIER** *into darkness, then stops.)*

Come back!

(Suddenly grabbing the notebook from his back pocket, he futilely tries to rip, then bends it, before chucking it into the trash can...head bowed and weeping, he turns and solemnly inches up to the yellow strip at the edge of the stage, where he teeters over the darkness he now glares into...sadness turning to rage, he hears an approaching subway, then purposefully leans over the edge. Clenching his fists, he begins to leap, just as lights quick fade to black...flickering lights and roar of passing subway... lights back up on **EVE**, *once again alone on the platform.)*

EVE. Damn it, Billy, why didn't you come to me first? You were *always* the one I went to when no one else cared.

*(***BILLY*** suddenly emerges upstage left, a pure white T-shirt now draping over his jeans, as he slowly approaches* **EVE** *from behind.)*

All those times I fought with Mom and Dad, the time Tony Abolofia asked Noreen Corcoran to the dance instead of me, or that time Tommy Flanagan called me a *moon-faced freak* and you just sat me down, wiped the tears from my face, looked into my swollen eyes and said...

*(***BILLY*** is now right behind her, a nurturing, brotherly smile on his beaming face.)*

BILLY. The moon was created by God to give people freaked out by stuff during the day something beautiful to see at night—

EVE & BILLY. And if dopey Tommy Flanagan doesn't get that, then his head is harder than the lifeless rock the moon is made of.

*(**BILLY** withdraws into the shadows.)*

EVE. Yeah, I smiled. *Of course* I smiled. You *always* made me smile, especially those times when all I wanted to do was disappear and die. *(She walks to the platform edge, looking up.)* So what am I supposed to do now, huh? Who do I turn to when *my* heart is broken, when *my* soul is crushed? Who fills the hole in *my* heart? I can't go back to school, Billy. How do I walk the same halls with the people who cursed and tormented you *without* ripping their faces off? How do I live under the same roof with the people who tossed away the one human being I loved more than anything or anyone in the entire world? You tell me, Billy, tell me why, instead of being home in my room, laying out my prettiest clothes for midnight mass, I'm standing here wondering why I shouldn't throw myself off this platform and follow you to wherever the hell you went! *You were always enough for me, Billy, why wasn't I enough for you?*

(She falls to her knees...the approaching rumble of oncoming subway is heard, then thunders by...flickering lights and roar fade...the trash can nearby rattles – she instantly recoils in fear....suddenly, the cooing, then crying, of an infant is heard...inching her way closer, she peers over, into, then slowly pulls herself up by the trash can opening. Furiously scooping aside the trash and newspapers, she suddenly stops when the source of the crying is uncovered.)

Oh my God!

(Reaching in, she gently removes a newspaper-covered, crying infant.)

What are you doing here?

(Kneeling, she peels away the newspapers, then cradles the baby while removing the jacket, one sleeve at a time, blanketing the infant with it.)

EVE. *(cont.)* Why aren't you home in your room, sound asleep in your crib like all the other babies?

(She clutches the suddenly screaming child against her.)

Alright, alright, I get it, no questions asked. *(She gently rocks it back and forth.)* You don't have to be afraid anymore, Evie's here.

(The infant eventually calms, then begins to coo.)

That's better...gee, you're one lucky...*(peeling away newspaper to get a closer look)* ...boy – lucky that I was here when I was. Then again, maybe we're *both* lucky, lucky we were *both* at the right station at just the right...

(cell phone suddenly rings)

...uh-oh, guess who *that* is.

(Removing the phone, she stares at it before flipping it open, as lights again come up down stage right on **MOTHER,** *holding the phone, and* **FATHER,** *now wearing a zippered windbreaker, anxiously pacing behind her.)*

MOTHER. Evie, it's me, are you there? Can you hear me? *Evie?*

FATHER. Is she saying anything?

MOTHER. Does it sound like she's saying anything? Evie!

FATHER. Let me speak to her.

MOTHER. No.

FATHER. That's it, Mary, I need to speak to her.

MOTHER. I said, not now.

FATHER. No, Mary... *(He pulls the phone away from her.)* ...now!

MOTHER. Give that back!

FATHER. Evie, it's me, it's Daddy.

MOTHER. You know she won't say anything to you.

FATHER. Please, baby, talk to me, *please! Evie?*

EVE. What.

FATHER. You're there! Thank God you're there!

MOTHER. She's talking?

FATHER. Please don't hang up.

MOTHER. Is she talking?

FATHER. We just want to know you're alright, honey, that you're safe.

EVE. Yeah, we're alright, I mean, *I'm* alright.

FATHER. Are you sure?

EVE. I'm fine, Daddy, really.

FATHER. Where are you?

EVE. Doesn't matter.

FATHER. You're right, it *doesn't* matter, because wherever you are I'll pick you up and bring you right back home.

EVE. No! I mean - I don't know - I'm not sure if I can—

FATHER. Evie, there's nothing I can ever do or say that can bring Billy back, and that fact will break my heart every second I have left on this earth, but maybe one day, if you give me half a chance, maybe I'll finally be able to learn how to be the Father you *both* deserved.

(Wincing, she stares into the eyes of the infant wiggling in her arms, both engulfed in the flickering lights of the express train now whistling by.)

FATHER. *(cupping the phone)* She's in the subway!

MOTHER. Oh, my God, my baby!

(Subway lights and rumble fade.)

FATHER. Evie, are you still there?

EVE. I'm here.

FATHER. Are you sure you're OK?

EVE. I said I'm...Daddy?

FATHER. What, honey?

EVE. Did you really mean that "no questions asked" stuff?

FATHER. *Absolutely!* It can be a fresh start, baby, a new beginning. Where are you now?

EVE. Not far.

FATHER. Please tell me where, I can jump in the car and—

EVE. No, you don't have to.

FATHER. But I *want* to.

EVE. Don't *push* so hard, Daddy, OK?

FATHER. Sure, baby, sure.

EVE. I can get home by myself, alright?

FATHER. But—

EVE. Alright?

FATHER. Anything you say, baby, just please be careful.

EVE. Bye.

(Lights out on **PARENTS** *as she closes cell and slides it back into the jacket pocket, all the while staring at the child in her arms.)*

So what do you think, little man, what should we do now?... *(Brushing the baby's face with her hand, she stands, then presents the infant outward and upward.)*...look at him, Billy, look how handsome he is, and can you believe it, he's got a moon face, just like...*(looks up with a knowing smile)*...very clever, big brother, very, very clever... *(back to baby)* ...guess we're just going to have to take you home, get you some food, clean you up, then try to find your Mommy, and if we can't do that, then, well – we'll see – hey, how'd you like to come to midnight mass with me? *(The infant begins to giggle.)* I'll take that as a yes...*(looking up, with that smile)*...You did it again, Billy, you *always* make me smile, and now you've even got *him* doin' it.

(She turns to leave, then kicks something in the pile of crinkled newspapers and trash. Reaching down, she pulls Billy's crumpled notebook from the pile. Looking up, she tries to smile through her tears.)

Thank you, Billy...*(clutching the baby and Billy's book to her chest)* Catch up with you later, ok?

(She turns and withdraws into darkness, just as another train roars through the now empty station.)

(blackout)

PUSH back! Crisis Lifeline Resource Guide

Below is a partial list of organizations that offer a wide range of immediate action, aid, assistance, and information on bullying, abuse, violence, and suicide prevention. Never forget - YOU ARE NOT ALONE!

- **NATIONAL BULLYING PREVENTION CENTER**

  PACER's *National Bullying Prevention Center* provides creative and interactive resources that are designed to benefit all students, including students with disabilities. Middle and high school students can visit www:PACERTeensAgainstBullying.org and elementary school students PACERKidsAgainstBuliying.org for additional ideas on how they can take action against bullying. www.pacer.org/bullying

- **THE TREVOR PROJECT**

  They run the *Trevor Lifeline*, a 24-hour, national crisis and suicide prevention lifeline for gay and questioning teens. The number is 1-866-4-U-TREVOR (1-866-488-7386). Learn more about The Trevor Project and the other great programs they have at: www.thetrevorproject.org

- **IT GETS BETTER PROJECT**

  Mission: Showing young LGBT people the levels of happiness, potential, and positivity their lives will reach if they can just get through their teen years. The *It Gets Better* Project wants to remind teenagers in the LGBT community that they are not alone - and it WILL get better. www.itgetsbetter.org

- **GLSEN**

  The *Gay, Lesbian & Straight Education Network* strives to assure that each member of every school community is valued and respected regardless of sexual orientation or gender identity/expression. www.glsen.org

- **RACHEL'S CHALLENGE**

  The first person killed at Columbine High School on April 20, 1999, Rachel Scott's acts of kindness and compassion coupled with the contents of her six diaries have become the foundation for one of the most life-changing school programs in America. Mission: "We exist to inspire, equip and empower every person to create a permanent positive culture change in their school, business and community by starting a chain reaction of kindness and compassion." www.rachelschallenge.org

- **RAINN**

  The *Rape, Abuse & Incest National Network* is the nation's largest anti-sexual violence organization. RAINN operates the National Sexual Assault Hotline at 1.800.656.HOPE and the National Sexual Assault Online Hotline at www.rainn.org, and publicizes the hotlines' free, confidential services; educates the public about sexual violence; and leads national efforts to prevent sexual violence, improve services to victims and ensure that rapists are brought to justice. One of "America's 100 Best Charities" - *Worth* magazine

- **THE TYLER CLEMENTI FOUNDATION**

  The parents of Rutgers student Tyler Clementi, who took his own life in 2010, have set up the Tyler Clementi Foundation under the creed "Live = Let Live." Mission: "To raise awareness of the issues surrounding, and support organizations concerned with, suicide prevention, acceptance of LGBT teens, and education against internet cyber bullying." www.TheTylerClementiFoundation.org

PROP/COSTUME LIST

Stage Props

Subway station sign

Bouquets of withering flowers, clustered beneath sign

Two red chairs

Red garbage can, filled with trash, crumpled newspapers, and a towel-wrapped baby doll

Costumes/Personal Props

EVE

A too large red varsity jacket (or any kind of red team jacket) embroidered with the name BILLY

Red woolen cap

Cell phone

Box cutter

Semi-stuffed wrinkled paper lunch bag

BILLY

Red varsity jacket, embroidered with the name BILLY, identical to Eve's

Red woolen cap

Well-used, rollable, marble notebook and pen

MOTHER

Typical house dress and red pocketed apron

Cell phone

FATHER

Blue collar work clothes, including wind breaker

Red napkin

TEENAGE GIRLS #1 & #2

Late fall garb of typical High School girls, some article of clothing must be red

School books and backpacks

TEENAGE BOY

Goth, grunge or any anti-jock look, with one red article of clothing

School books and back pack

JAVIER

Suavely dressed for late fall, with red shirt

HOODIED FIGURE

Black hoodie and pants

APPENDIX

This was the original monologue from which PUSH evolved. It was first performed, with Miss Emma Charap originating the role of Eve, on December 14, 2010, at the Producers Club in NYC.

CHRISTMAS EVE AT THE ESPLANADE

By George Cameron Grant

(Scene: Esplande subway station, Bronx.)

(Time: 5am, Christmas Eve.)

(At rise: **EVE**, *a girl of 16, sits huddled in a corner of the subway station, sound asleep, hands stuffed into the pockets of the way too big varsity jacket she wears, matching wool cap pulled over the flowing brown hair covering her shoulders. The thunder of an oncoming express train is heard, and as it passes, its lights throw the stirring* **EVE** *into a kaleidoscope of strobing lights. As the roar of the train fades, she nuzzles deeper into the corner, just as the clanking of a garbage can cover is heard. Eyes instantly open, she springs to her feet, hands emerging from the jacket, one holding an open box cutter now extended and ready for anything...)*

EVE. Who's there? I know you're hiding behind that pole, so you might as well come out where I can see you!... *(cautiously approaching the pole)* ...I'm warning you, I've got a sharp blade in my hand and I'm not afraid to use it, so if you're thinking of trying anything, you'd better... *(the sound of running footsteps)* ...jeez, it's just a...hey, come back, I thought you were just another creep trying to...really, you don't have to run away!... *(closing the box cutter, she pockets it)* ...I put it away, see? I'm not going to hurt you, I swear. If you're hungry, I've got half a sandwich here somewhere... *(removing a wrapped half-sandwich, she extends it)* ...see, here it is, now come back! Hey!

(She stuffs the sandwich back into the jacket pocket...)

She's gone... *(She looks up.)* ...damn it, Billy, you happy now? Do you see what's goin' on down here? You've got me scarin' the hell out of some kid more frightened than I am! Look, I don't mean to yell at you, but everything's such a freakin' mess. I'm a mess, Mom and Dad are a mess, it's all turned to crap, and I don't know what to do or who else to turn to, so you're just gonna' have to put up with it, OK? Why did you have to do this, Billy, huh?

(Slowly returning to the corner, she slides to the floor...)

I remember the exact moment you told me. Thanksgiving morning in front of the TV, right before the parade came on. I knew you'd been holding something in, but I never would have guessed...my big brother in love! I was so happy, you have to believe that, and I'd never seen you so excited, but I also knew you well enough to feel something different than the words you were saying, all that time you were smiling I had the feeling something was wrong, and then you said the word that changed everything. Javier. I know you kept talking after that, but it had to be ten minutes before I could hear what you were saying, because all I could do was keep playing that name over and over in my head...Javier...Javier...Javier...hoping maybe it would change to Jessica, Juanita, Johanna, anything but...Billy, I've never been closer to anyone in my entire life, so how come I didn't know this, never sensed it, suspected it, not even for a second? I mean, it's not like you didn't go out with girls, and not like any girl you didn't go out with wouldn't have committed murder to go out with you, so how come every time you'd tell me about your dates I never realized there was something wrong, how come it never occurred to me that what was missing in your eyes was what I saw that morning when you said...the word. Could it be you never knew it yourself? Maybe you did you know it, but had to deny your feelings until you found someone you couldn't deny? Or maybe you were just too afraid to say anything because you knew what everyone's reaction would be?

(A cell phone rings…)

Well, well, there they are again, good old Mom and Dad. They call me every 10 minutes. Usually I don't pick up, but if I do, I only listen. I never make a sound. "Please come back, baby, we miss you terribly. We're sorry for everything we said, everything we did. We need you, Emily, now more than ever, we can't bear the thought of losing two children, we just want you back, baby, no questions asked." Blah, blah, blah, blah! Big of them, huh? But what about my questions?… *(into the silent phone)* …Like how do you spit in your own son's face when he tells you he's in love?… *(looking up, whispering)* …OK, so Thanksgiving dinner might not have been the best time to break the news… *(back into phone)* …but how do you throw him to the curb without a change of clothes, tell him not to bother coming back home because the locks will be changed, then actually change them?…Huh?…Huh?… *(stuffs the phone into the jacket pocket)* …So maybe you already know this, and maybe you don't, but the story's everywhere… TV, newspapers, radio, all over the freakin' internet. Teen subway tragedy! Troubled honor student jumps to his death! Troubled! Can you believe that crap? Everyone thinks they know you, think they know what happened, but I know the truth. You didn't jump, not really, you were pushed. Every time you heard those other words…faggot, fairy, fruit… *(she pushes toward track)* …push! When Mom and Dad turned their backs on you and tossed you out… *(pushes again)* …push! Or when Javier told you that the whole mess was just too much of a hassle and that he needed space, like 5000 miles worth… *(gently pushes outward)* …push. Just another set of hands pushing you to this spot and onto those tracks. Look, I get it, but damn it, Billy, why didn't you come to me first? You were always the one I went to when no one else cared. All those times I fought with Mom and Dad, the time Tony Abolofia asked Noreen Corcoran to the dance instead of me, or when Tommy Flanagan called me a moon-faced freak and you just sat me down, wiped the tears from my face, looked into my swollen eyes and told me how the moon was created by God to give the people freaked out by stuff during the day something beautiful to see at night, and if dopey Tommy Flanagan didn't get that, then his head was harder than the lifeless rock the moon was made of. Yeah, I smiled. Sure I smiled. You always made me smile, especially the times when all I wanted to do was disappear and die, so what am I supposed to do now? Who do I turn to when my heart is broken, when my soul is crushed? Who fills the hole in my heart? I can't go back to school, Billy. How do I walk the same halls with the people who cursed and tormented you without ripping their faces off? How do I live under the same roof with the same people who threw away the one human being I loved more than anything or anyone in the world without locking them in the basement and leaving them to rot? You tell me, Billy, tell me why, instead of being home in my room, laying out my prettiest clothes for midnight mass, I'm standing here wondering why I shouldn't throw myself off this platform and follow you to wherever the hell you went! You were always enough for me, Billy, why wasn't I enough for you?

(She moves dangerously close to the platform edge as the approaching rumble of an oncoming train is heard, then thunders by, as she falls to her knees…lights and roar fade just as the waste can down platform left from her suddenly rattles…startled, she turns to it, just as the cooing, then crying, of an infant is heard…running to the can, she rips off the cover, gasps, then reaches in,

*gently removing a newspaper-covered crying infant...
lowering the baby to the floor, she removes the sweatshirt
and spreads it out before cocooning the infant within...
clutching the bundled child against her, she gently rocks
it back and forth...)*

Oh, my God, what are you doing here? You should
home in your crib fast asleep... *(The baby screams.)* ...
Alright, OK, I get it, no questions asked...you don't
have to be afraid anymore, baby, Emily's here. You're
safe now, no one can hurt you... *(The infant begins to
calm, then coos.)* ...ah, now that's better. Wow, you sure
are one lucky baby that I was here when I was. Come to
think of it, maybe I was luckier. Maybe we were both at
the right station at just the right time.

*(Cell phone suddenly rings...removing it, she stares at it
before reluctantly opening it...)*

Hello?...Yeah, it's me, we're alright...I mean, I'm
alright...really, I'm fine...I don't know...I'm not
sure...not sure I can...*(looks at baby)*...well, um...uh...
did you really mean that "no questions asked" stuff?...
Not far...no, you don't have to, I can get there by
myself...have to think about it...don't push me, daddy,
alright?...Alright?...Bye.

*(She closes the cell and slides it back into the jacket pocket
before staring at the child in her arms...)*

...so what do you think, little one, what should we
do?... *(brushing the baby's face with her hand, she then
extends her outward)* ...look at her, Billy, how pretty is
she? And would you believe it, she's got a moon face,
just like... *(looks up)* ...oh, very clever, big brother, very,
very clever... *(back to the baby)* ...I guess we're just going
to have to take you home, get you some food, clean
you up, then try to find your Mommy, and if we can't
do that, then, well, we'll see...hey, would you like to
come to midnight mass with me?

(The infant begins to giggle...)

I'll take that as a yes... *(looking up, with an ever so slight smile)* ...You did it again. You always make me smile. Thank you, Billy. Maybe we'll catch up with you later, OK?

(Standing, she clutches the baby to her chest and exits, as another train roars through the now empty station...)

(blackout)

ABOUT THE AUTHOR

GEORGE CAMERON GRANT is an internationally produced author of eight full length plays, over twenty one acts, and numerous monologues. His latest one act play PUSH joins EPITAPH, a full-length play dedicated to his Father, and 4 X'MAS, his evening of one-act Christmas plays, as published members of the Samuel French family. He is an eight-time Samuel French Off Off Broadway Short Play Festival Finalist, most recently in 2009 for his play FORECLOSURE, which was also named a Finalist in the Nantucket Short Play Festival. PUSH was a Semi-Finalist in NYC's 2011 Strawberry Festival, garnering Best Actress and Best Director nominations. The Eastside Players of Madison (WI) High School entered PUSH into the 2012 Wisonsin High School Theatre Festival, receiving an All-State Award, and an Outstanding Actor Award for Scout Slava-Ross' portrayal of Eve. LEBEN, his full-length taking on pro-life/pro-choice issues, had its West Coast Premiere September 2012, at the Stage Door Repertory Theatre in Anaheim, CA. His new full-length Christmas play, HEAVEN CENT, written on commission for the same theater, had its World Premiere there on November, 2012, and was called "ONE OF THE YEAR'S 5 BEST" by Angela Hatcher of the Orange County News.

As Bookwriter/Lyricist/Composer, George recently completed a hugely successful series of staged readings of IN SEARCH OF ALICE, the second original musical he has created in collaboration with New York composer Michael J. Shapiro.

Also a two-time participant in the NY Independent Film Market, George has just completed his fourth screenplay DOUBLE EXPOSURE.

Composer of dozens of songs, George's PASS ON THE LOVE, performed by the legendary Persuasions, was featured in Spike Lee's DO IT A CAPPELLA.

George is an Addy Award winner for his graphic design work on August Wilson's FENCES, also creating for scores of motion pictures, including Academy Award® Winners and Nominees including ANVIL-THE STORY OF ANVIL, MONSTER, Y TU MAMA TAMBIEN, WHALE RIDER and AMADEUS.

George is the proud father of Elizabeth and Jenna. He is a member of BMI and the Dramatists Guild.

He can be reached on Facebook, Twitter: @cameron313, email: cameron313@aol.com or at www.georgecamerongrant.com.

Also by
George Cameron Grant...

4 X'MAS

Epitaph

OTHER GEORGE CAMERON GRANT TITLES
AVAILABLE FROM SAMUEL FRENCH

4 X'MAS
George Cameron Grant

Comedy/Drama/Fantasy

THE OFFICE PARTY *(2m, 1f)* - Bill and Joyce meet at a holiday office party, rekindling a love affair that leads to Joyce's living room and the possible early arrival of Richard, the third side of an unresolved triangle.

SANTA'S CLARA *(2m, 1f)* - In the shadows of a Hell's Kitchen bottle redemption center, a fired department store Santa meets a teenage runaway toting a shopping cart of empties and a cynical heart full of nightmare-shrouded sugar plum memories. But tonight, more than bottles may get redeemed.

THE FIRST NOEL *(1f)* - A homeless and hungry Noel returns to the site of her childhood, now a Chinese take-out, but will her journey get her the handout she wants, or the nurturing she needs?

BALLS *(4f, 1m)* - A box of very eccentric, multi-colored holiday ornaments discover just how fragile their existence really is.

SANTA COMES TO THE KING DAVID *(3f, 1m)* - A distraught woman saves what she thinks is a bridge leaper in a Santa suit, discovering instead a story of unfulfilled dreams, unconditional devotion, a Kris Kringle who makes annual visits to a Jewish nursing home, and the crazy possibility that two broken hearts can indeed make one whole.

OTHER GEORGE CAMERON GRANT TITLES AVAILABLE FROM SAMUEL FRENCH

EPITAPH

George Cameron Grant

Drama/Fantasy / 7m, 2f

Awarded the Catholic Writer's Guild Seal of Approval!

Returning to the unmarked grave of his long-deceased father, Winston is determined to finally have carved into stone what he could never put into words. There he's met by C, a surprisingly young, beautiful, and very female mason, who helps him discover that before anyone can sum up a life, they first have to look at that life, and their own, honestly.

Lightning Source UK Ltd.
Milton Keynes UK
UKHW021258171022
410616UK00025B/485

9 780874 403312